A VERY
TWISTED
TALE

Berry Halpin

Book design by Halpin Enterprises
Cover design by Halpin Enterprises

ISBN - Paperback: 9798872073956
First Edition: December 202 3

CONTENTS

1

Hansel
& Gretel

Once upon a time there lived two children - a girl and a boy. Gretel, the girl, was nine and was always coming up with crazy ideas. Hansel, her brother, was the same age and was 'not afraid of anything.' The children lived together, deep in the forest.

Hansel's tummy rumbled, so Gretel collected some berries for them to share. As Hansel nibbled on the tasty treat, he began to shiver. Gretel covered him in a fern leaf because his lips were turning blue.

As the moon came up, with their tummies full of berries, Hansel and Gretel began to nod off. Just then, they heard a noise coming from a nearby bush.

"Wh...wh...what was that?" asked Hansel, his eyes wide.

"Maybe it's just the wind?" Gretel replied, looking around.

Suddenly, out of nowhere, came a girl wearing a red hood. "WOLF!" she yelled. "RUN! HIDE! NOW!"

2

Little Red Riding Hood

Hansel and Gretel jumped up and ran after the girl in the red hood. They huddled together behind a huge oak tree, trying to catch their breath. A howl pierced the air. It was definitely a wolf. The children looked at each other. Hansel gulped.

Just then, a woodcutter came striding through the forest. He spotted the children huddled together. "Are you lot alright?" he asked.

The trio came out looking frightened. "We didn't do anything," Hansel blurted out.

"I know you didn't," the Woodcutter replied. "It was all that nasty wolf. I wish B.A.D had never been invented."

"What's B.A.D?" Gretel asked.

The woodcutter laughed. He looked at the girl in the red hood and said, "Are you going to tell them, or shall I?"

"They need to know," she said.

Hansel and Gretel turned to face the girl in the red hood. "Listen up you two. This is important."

The girl told them that her name was Little Red Riding Hood - but her friends called her Red. She explained that B.A.D was the Bridge Trolls and Demons Network – an underground gang of bad guys including Big Wolf and Bad Wolf.

The Woodcutter began building a fire as Red ushered Hansel and Gretel to sit on her cloak, closer to the fire. Red shared ghastly tales of the B.A.D network. How they had nearly made a cheesecake base out of the Gingerbread Man; how they had sewn open Snow White's eyelids so that she could never sleep and meet her Prince; and, how they had stapled the Frog Prince's feet to a lily pad so he's forever floating in the middle of the lake.

Hansel and Gretel gasped at all the gory details. It was clear that the B.A.D Network had been up to no good. Red explained how they'd been trying to infiltrate the gang for a while but had not been able to stop them wreaking havoc - and they were still at large.

Somewhere in the distance, a wolf howled.

They huddled closer, thinking about their close encounter with the B.A.D Network. With their faces warmed by the fire, and their tummies nourished by the pies and cakes from Red's basket, Hansel gently leant to one side as if he was going to whisper something important to Red. Instead, he farted. A loud, wet, stinky fart.

"You're so gross!" said Gretel as she wafted away the smell.

"Delicious food Red. So rich. My stomach is not used to such delights - do excuse me."

3

The Plan

After Red had finished recounting the awful tales of the B.A.D network, Hansel and Gretel knew they had to do something.

"What's the plan?" asked Gretel. "You have got a plan, haven't you?"

"No way. We've tried already. Not even the strongest knight in the Kingdom could defeat them. We have no chance against them," replied the Woodcutter.

"But we can't just give up!" exclaimed Gretel. "Otherwise, it'll be us next. We had a close shave with the wolf back there. And something tells me he'll be back."

Gretel convinced them that they needed to make a plan to bring down the B.A.D network. She was sure it was the only way they would at least have a shot at beating them. So, they put their heads together and started scheming. Before long, they had come up with a simple but fool proof plan.

THE PLAN

Step 1: Find people to join their crew.
Step 2: Find out where the B.A.D Network were hiding out.
Step 3: Crush them!

They were proud of their new plan. Now they just needed to put it into action.

Proud and tired, they decided to get some sleep. As they settled down and closed their eyes, the Woodcutter headed back to his cottage in the woods.

4

Jack & The Beanstalk

Hansel, Gretel and Red woke up early the next morning and began their daily routines. Red's was by far the most eccentric.

- put on a cloak
- whip up a batch of breakfast muffins
- leave out a bowl of biscuits for the local stray
- do 25 push-ups
- hug a tree

"So that bit of our plan where it jumps from Step 2 to Step 3? I think we need Step 2a, 2b, c, d, e, f, g, h, i, j, k, l, m...." Hansel said, his voice getting higher and higher until Gretel covered his mouth with her hand.

"Stop overthinking things", said Gretel. "Do you think Jack stopped to write a 50-page executive plan or deploy a full risk assessment before he scaled the beanstalk?"

"Speaking of beanstalks..." gestured Red. And there, straight ahead, was a huge green beanstalk, towering over them.

The stalk went up into the clouds for what seemed like miles. Gretel and Red headed towards the beanstalk, with Hansel reluctantly following them, wishing they would at least *listen* to his concerns on potential beanstalk rot.

Without warning, there came an earth-shattering stomp, which shook the ground beneath them. Then they heard a blood-curdling scream - "Giiiiiiiiiaaaaant!!!" and saw a boy running manically towards them.

He was grasping a Golden Harp and a Goose's head was poking out of the top of his rucksack. In unison, they all turned and ran with the boy until they were safely concealed in a nearby cave.

"Hi! I'm Hansel, this is Gretel and she's..."

The boy interrupted "Shhh! No - he'll hear you. Please - just answer me this - your ancestors aren't from England, are they??"

"No – Germany," - whispered Gretel.

"China," added Red.

"Thank God for that. If anyone's getting eaten it's me then," said the boy. "I'm Jack by the way."

"Clearly," said Gretel. "Is this the famous golden egg laying goose?"

"The one and only Cluckers," replied Jack. "Terrible conditions he keeps his pets in up there. RSPCA guidelines say they must have access to outdoor space. This poor thing hasn't seen any sunlight in years."

"Finally - someone who respects rules as much as I do," Hansel rejoiced.

"Well, I don't know about that. I tried chaining myself to the beanstalk to start with - turns out the giant wasn't so fussed. I just hate seeing animals treated badly."

He carefully pulled a bunch of clover from his top pocket and fed it to Quackers.

"My Grandma used to say you were nothing more than a common thief. I didn't know you were an animal activist," said Red, looking at Jack in admiration.

"It's a common misconception. It's the harp you see. No one understands why I steal the harp. It's because Quackers wont sleep for love nor money without it. I have no interest in gold and riches. I just want a better life for animals."

Quackers gobbled on the clover and waggled his tail.

"You must be Little Red? My mum used to say you were a few sandwiches short of a picnic. I mean, a wolf, disguised as your Grandma?! You *really* should have gone to Specsavers."

Red's face went red as her temper bubbled to her cheeks. She launched her basket at Jack.

"Hey, hey, hey! We're the good guys remember?" pleaded Hansel.

"You don't need to tell me that." said Jack.

"What we mean to say is...", said Gretel trying to mediate, "...we need each other. We need to defeat B.A.D. We need you, Jack. And you, Red - glasses or no glasses."

5

The Gingerbread Man

The newfound friends found that they shared a common goal. To defeat B.A.D - whatever it took. They continued their journey into the countryside, nearing a farm.

Gretel rubbed her eyes furiously as she stared into the distance. "Hansel! Do you see what I see?"

Hansel looked over the field and could see what looked like a huge gingerbread house with a fox's tail sticking out of the sugar paper window.

"HELP!" screamed a high-pitched voice.

"Someone must be in trouble!" exclaimed Red.

"Count us OUT!" stated Gretel matter-of-factly. Hansel gave a supportive nod.

"Oh - Gingerbread house. Of course." nodded Red.

They looked around and Jack was already speeding across the field. "The poor fox is stuck!"

"JACK!!!! Did no-one read to that boy?? Come on you two - we can't let him and Quackers face a hungry fox alone. Remember - we need each other!"

Hansel and Gretel reluctantly followed as Red took off across the field after Jack.

As Jack neared the house, Quackers began flapping furiously in his backpack, so much so, he sent Jack into a spin. "What's wrong Quackers? Stop! We need to help poor fox!"

Quackers, terrified by the site of the fox, pecked, flapped, spat, shrieked, and pecked some more. At the same time the tiniest gingerbread figure came bolting out of the house.

"Silly old Fox. You can't catch me, I'm the Gingerbread Man."

In his excitement, the Gingerbread Man showcased his gymnastics prowess, somersaulting into a split jump, bouncing up into a scissor leap, and a triple wolf turn, before back-flipping into a perfect round off and proudly taking a bow right in front of Red, Hansel and Gretel.

Subconsciously, Hansel licked his lips and his tummy let out an all too familiar rumble.

"Don't even think about it!" Gretel said, hitting Hansel in the tummy.

"You'll be safe in here little one," said Red affectionately. She lifted the Gingerbread Man into her basket. "Wonderful gymnastics!" she said.

"Why thank you. I've been working on that wolf turn for a while" he said, with a curtsey.

"Could you teach me?" asked Red.

Meanwhile, Jack had finally managed to calm Quackers by jumping in the pond.

"You alright in there?" Gretel asked, holding back her giggles.

"I don't know what came over him, but my old mum used to say feed 'em, bath 'em or turn 'em upside down."

"I think you'll find it was the fox that made Quackers, well...quackers," said Gretel pointing at the blur of orange speeding away into the woods.

"Come on, let's go!" said Red.

"Where's Hansel?" Gretel face-palmed her head. "Hansel! Stop eating that house!! That boy never learns."

"Aw maaan," said Hansel "But the gingerbread is really delicious".

.

6

Goldilocks & her Army of Bears

Overcome by the sweet aromatic smell of freshly baked gingerbread, the group rubbed their bellies in hunger. "Please can we stop somewhere to eat?" pleaded a hungry Jack.

"No! We must keep going," instructed Red. "They're gaining ground and we can't give up just because we're hungry." Red was holding the food basket, so she had the final say.

They carried on walking, when suddenly Jack began sniffing the air. "Oh my...I can smell cinnamon porridge...and...and...cranberry jam." He swooned, licking his lips and wafting the smell towards his nose.

"He's hallucinating with hunger" sighed Red.

Hansel sniffed the air. "No, I can smell it too!"

"And if I'm not mistaken, there's some nutmeg in there too!" the Gingerbread man chimed in with authority.

"Porridge!" they all screamed with delight.

"Come on guys, let's follow the smell!" said Gretel, charging to the front.

"Hang on a minute!" said Hansel. "Shouldn't we check if anyone has an oat allergy?"

But Hansel was alone in his worries and realised he had better follow or be left behind once again.

They approached the cottage, with the smell of sweet porridge getting stronger - and the noise of their rumbling bellies, getting louder.

On the gate they noticed a sign saying, 'No poking!'. Hansel gulped. Above the open cottage door, a sign read 'Just Right Café."

"The door is open," said Gretel encouragingly.

"Come on!" said Jack. "My shout."

They sat at a large round table with seats of various sizes. Hansel hesitantly took the last seat, which had seen better days. The chair legs buckled under his weight sending him tumbling to the floor.

Three bears and a girl with golden hair jumped up from behind the counter, laughing hysterically.

"We're sorry," said the girl, hitting the counter with her hand. "Never fails to make us laugh, that."

"Classic!" said the littlest bear.

As the girl wiped away her tears of laughter, she pulled her order pad and pencil from her apron and prepared to write. "Good news is, you've earned our daily special porridge. Big bowl for the price of a small bowl."

Hansel stood up gingerly, rubbing his back as he tried to smile along. He soon forgot the pain and became fixated on her huge sharp claws, as she dropped a large rocking chair behind him and signalled for him to sit.

"We'll have four of the specials please and just a few dry oats for Quackers if that's ok?" said Jack.

"Coming right up." She disappeared into the kitchen.

The smallest bear introduced himself. "I'm Little bear" he said and then pointed over to the larger bears. "That's Mummy bear and that's Daddy bear.

"In the forest where my grandma lives, everyone calls you Baby Bear," said Red.

"Well, after I scared Goldilocks half to death, we all decided that Little Bear suited me better."

Suddenly, the girl re-emerged from the kitchen with her hands on her hips. "That wicked witch! She's only gone and stolen our oats again!" exclaimed Goldilocks. "What does she do with them? Little! Can you pop to the Windmill please?"

Goldilocks looked thoroughly fed up as she handed Little the last few coins from the till. "We'll never be able to keep to this cafe afloat if that horrid witch continues stealing our food."

"Karma" whispered Jack to Quackers.

Red shot Jack a silencing glance and seized the opportunity to recruit Goldilocks to join their mission

'Forge a cunning and courageous plan to defeat B.A.D - the baddest baddies this side of Badville' (and also: to think of a shorter name for it!).

As the newly formed gang set off for Badville, a giant, jet-powered pumpkin soared past them at breakneck speed. They all look at each other and said "Cinders!"

"Let's follow that pumpkin," charged Gretel.

"Urm... didn't work out so well for us, last time we followed a food trail..." warned Hansel.

"Not the time Hansel - NOT the time!" she retorted.

7

Cinderella

Ignoring Hansel's complaints, they began to run after the pumpkin, following the trail to a very old, crooked-looking house. They knocked on the battered wooden door.

"Cinders!" said a croaky high-pitched voice, "Get the door or you'll be scraping the wax off the candle holders all night."

Then a tall girl with scruffy hair and goggles appeared at the door. "Who are..." but, before she could finish her sentence, a deafeningly loud BANG came from the upstairs room.

"That will be the solar powered catapult I've been working on," she said, as she opened the door wide and beckoned them to follow her up the creaky staircase.

Gingerbread man creaked his neck, looking at all the bottles and potions and bubbling experiments lining every table, bookshelf and chair in the room. He gulped as he spotted the extra-large jar of Bicarbonate of Soda, backing away from the workbench and fearful that he may become her next experiment.

"Don't worry Ginge. Your bicarb has already been activated - and that's a huge tub up there!", comforted Red.

"Take no notice of all my experiments – they're just something to keep me busy! I HATE sewing and cleaning! My latest work in progress is THIS beauty!" She pointed proudly to a weird contraption on the table. "This is the super-duper-never-have-to-set-the-table-again-catapult. Onto my 32nd dining set now, but you know what they say..."

"33rd time a charm?" asked Jack with a sly smile.

"Exactly!" grinned Cinderella.

Gretel felt in her bones that Cinderella could be an important member of their effort to free Fairytale Island.She explained their mission to Cinders who accepted the opportunity at once.

Suddenly, there was a loud knock at the door that sent shockwaves through the house. Cinders looked terrified and Quackers nearly jumped out of her feathers.

The gang understood in an instant what the deafening sound meant. Quickly, they all hid under the work bench. Cinders braced herself for what was about to happen.

The door burst open. In walked a tall woman with brown, beady eyes, crumpled teeth and pursed pointed lips. Her thin crooked neck faltering under the weight of her pearly necklace. She towered over Cinders, her voice booming out. "WHAT have I told you about these pots and potions?"

"To bring them to the dump Stepmother" replied Cinders weakly.

"Then WHY do I have neighbours calling me to say my house has exploded? WHY are there pots and potions everywhere? You are on borrowed time girl." She flicked her cloak, sending potions spinning off the table and across the floor.

Amidst the furore, Goldilocks worked quietly in the corner, bending and moulding her porridge spoons - determined to fix the catapult. She opened the control panel to a sea of buttons in all colours and sizes. She mouthed "Which colour?" to Cinders.

But Cinders was under the watchful eye of her horrid stepmother. She dared not to draw attention to Goldilocks or any of the gang.

"You're right, Stepmother. I am Rediculous. You ought to send me to REDDing, for being so Rediculous."

Goldi understood the message and pressed the red button, pointing the catapult arms in the direction of the wicked stepmother. The arms stretched out, grabbed the stepmother, rolled her into a ball shape, before firing her almost 100 meters into the air.

The stepmother gave out a blood-curdling scream. "CINDERS – YOU'LL PAY FOR THIS!"

"Run?" asked Cinders. They all nodded in agreement. The three bears grabbed the robot catapult and sped out of the house.

8

Billy, Goat & Gruff

F ree from the wicked Stepmother for now, Cinders was embracing her newfound freedom. "Come on guys! Let's play Pooh Sticks on this bridge."

Everyone searched for a stick and headed onto the bridge. Hansel was checking the bridge weight capacity sign when a loud voice boomed, "Who's that trip-trapping over my bridge?"

"You've GOT to be kidding me!" sighed Gretel.

"Quick! Follow us..." yelled three goats nearby.

Gretel grabbed Hansel and they all rushed across the bridge.

"Hi, I'm Billy, that's Gruff - and over there's Goat," said the first goat.

"Thanks for helping us make such a quick getaway," said Jack. Quackers squawked her agreement.

Goldilocks explained their ambitious plan to bring down the B.A.D Network for good. They all agreed the more, the merrier – and that the goats could be important members of their gang.

It had been a long day. After a quick snack, they began to settle down, ready to go to sleep - when they heard a low, grumbling sound.

"What in Giant Land is THAT!?" asked Jack, his eyes wide.

"Don't make a sound - it's the Bridge-Troll." Gruff whispered. "I thought we'd lost him."

"We need to get out of here," said Billy He's been following our scent trail, which means he's hungry."

"I've got an idea. I can maybe reboot the catapult into a get-away motor! You guys will need to build a raft though." Cinderella said.

"THAT ISN'T VERY SAFE!" Hansel shouted.

"SSSSSSSSSSHHHHHHHHHH!" they all whispered in unison.

Hansel knew by the look Gretel was giving him that they were going to do it - with or without him - but he was having no part in building a death device. He sat in the rushes as the rest of the crew started building a makeshift raft.

With Cinder's engineering prowess and Jack's handy woodwork skills, the catapult had been transformed into an outboard motor. Using strips of Red's cloak, they tied the motor onto the wonky raft and Cinders pulled the cable to jumpstart the engine.

"Phut phut phut" the motor sputtered but wouldn't start.

She looked panicked. Jack took a turn. Nothing.

The group were balanced precariously on the raft, as the low grumble became a loud tremor – the troll was getting closer. Meanwhile, Hansel was still refusing to get on board.

Gretel gave it one last try. "Hansel. Risk assess this: wobbly raft with a cranky engine (no offense Cinders) OR eaten alive by a hungry bridge troll? Alone! Here! By yourself! Did I say ALONE?"

Suddenly, the motor started. Gretel looked at Hansel and shouted "JUUUUUMP!"

Hansel took a running leap and landed on the edge of the raft, grabbing Daddy Bear's paw to get aboard. There was slight panic as the raft teetered back and forth – but soon the group found their balance and Jack gave a nod.

Cinderella jerked the engine into action, as Little Bear squealed "THE TROLL!" An ugly, wart-infested, swamp-smelling troll stomped towards the water's edge, eyeing them hungrily.

But they need not have worried. Cinder's boat slid into fifth gear and was streaming across the river to safety. (Well, as safe as anywhere this story is going to take them).

"What a beautiful view!" said Red.

"Yes – it's a beautiful horizon," agreed Jack.

"Horizon? - I think you mean Water faaaaaaaaaaaaaaaaaallllllllllllllllllllllllll!!"

The crew plunged down the ravine and into the lake below. Clambering out and soaked to the bone, they spotted Ginge lying flat on a rock. He was like a biscuit that had been dipped in hot tea for longer than it should. Even a Penguin biscuit wouldn't have survived a dip like that.

"Do we touch him?" whispered Red.

"No, absolutely NOT!" yelled Goldi.

"DR ABC" shouted Hansel.

"No! We need to dry him and quick!" Jack got a fire started and everyone huddled round, silently praying that Ginge would recover in the heat of the fire.

Ginge lay motionless. The smell of sweet ginger brought a tear to Red's eye as she turned away, unable to watch her friend in such a bad way.

Everyone hung their heads, accepting that the waterfall had taken their dear friend.

Then, just as Jack started to hum 'The Last Post,' a shower of golden syrup burst out of Ginge's mouth. He was ok!

The group cheered and danced as Ginge baked himself back to life.

.

9

Sleeping Beauty

After jumps of joy and sheer elation at Ginge's recovery (and a very sticky clean-up operation in the river), the group continued towards their final destination: Badville.

Entering the woodland, Hansel abruptly silenced everyone. "Shhh. Listen! Can you hear that thumping? It's the Troll. I knew they could swim! Run everyone! RUNNNNN!!"

With the trauma of nearly losing Ginge so fresh in everyone's minds, they darted quickly for cover. Quackers had different ideas. He wrangled himself free from Jack's backpack and started waddling joyously in the direction of the terrifying thumping sound.

"Quackers! No! Please come back," pleaded Jack.

Quackers continued undeterred - he seemed excited, happy even. Did he not realise he was waddling right into the menacing jaws of the Bridge Troll? Quackers waddled out of sight as the others held their breath.

Suddenly they heard shrieking quacks, quick and loud. Jack couldn't sit back and let his dear friend face a fate worse than death. He jumped from behind his rock and ran over the brook of the hill to rescue his friend.

"Jack, no! Come back!" Gretel shouted.

She looked around - everyone looked glum and defeated. Maybe they were out of their league attempting to take on the evil forces of B.A.D.

"Guys!" shouted Jack. "You will not believe this! Get over here!"

They clambered out from their mossy hiding spots and ran over the hill to join Jack, as a beautiful rose garden came into view. Beyond it, nestled a gorgeous little cottage that looked as if it was from a fairytale.

As they ventured closer, they saw a girl who looked like a princess, playing basketball. She stopped to give Quackers a huge hug. Finally, he came quacking back to them.

"Hi guys! Your goose is sweeter than the sugar plumb fairy! What's his name?" asked the girl.

"Quackers." said Jack feeling important.

"I'm Aurora, AKA Sleeping Beauty." said the girl.

"Cool! I've heard about how you pricked your finger on a spinning wheel in one of my Be Safe magazines," said Hansel.

After they had all introduced themselves, Aurora invited them to stay the night at her cottage. They were so grateful for a warm house and soft beds. It had been quite a journey already – and they were determined to complete their mission.

So, once they had all finished a delicious serving of Jellybean Stew (cooked by two marvellously talented fairies) they all snuggled under there blankets and went to sleep.

.

10

The Three
Little Pigs

The next morning, Aurora's fairies cooked scrambled dragon eggs for breakfast.

"I wonder who we might meet today?" asked Little Bear.

"Well, it won't be Belle I'm afraid. She is on a gap year travelling with Beast. And Rapunzel has just launched a new salon in High Tower Valley. And Snow White has moved to the Big Apple to go to law school", said Aurora.

"Well, she is the fairest of them all, I suppose," nodded Jack.

Just then, there was a loud banging at the door. The fairies opened the door to three panic-stricken pigs. They rushed into the living room, trying to catch their breath. "Lock the windows, lock the doors!" they shrieked.

The group did as they asked. As the pigs recovered, they introduced themselves to the group. The largest pig explained "I'm Twirly. Over there is Snouty and the one with the crossed eyes is Snorty."

Red asked, "What on EARTH were you running away from?" The pigs looked at each other, visibly shaken, and then told the group of the very real danger, lurking beyond the rose garden.

"We were just minding our own business, when we heard a loud knock on each of our doors. Then we heard the most unusual beat-box rapping rhymes saying:

"Little pigs, little pigs, let me come in!
I've been waiting outside - and eating from a bin
But I need a good meal that's not rotting kale
So don't be afraid - I'm only weak and frail!"

"His rap was so brilliant, and he sounded so HUNGRY that we each opened our doors - only to be faced with the most fearsome beast of a big bad wolf that we had ever seen! He tricked us and we only just escaped with our tails!"

Gretel decided to tell the pigs about their plan to destroy B.A.D. – after all, they'd just escaped from one of the biggest baddies ever (even if he could spit good rhymes). They instantly agreed to join the mission - but they all agreed that the plan to CRUSH THEM needed to be fleshed out.

.

11
CRUSH THEM
(in more detail)

Drawing on the special talents of each member of the crew, the plan of attack began to take shape:

- Step 1: Lure them in with porridge cooked by Goldilocks and the Three Bears
- Step 2: Drop one of Aurora's flowery soft bed sheets over them
- Step 3: Enter Goats to tap dance on their heads
- Step 4: Use Cinder's brilliant Catapult to fire jelly beans at them
- Step 5: Shoot them through a basketball hoop
- Step 6: Lay bricks at top speed to block them in

The plan was set.

The team was ready.

It was time to take down the B.A.D Network – once and for all.

.

12

The war to end all wars

They found the perfect spot. Everything was ready. Hansel had just completed the final risk assessment, but he still had a bad feeling in his gut – and it wasn't because of Goldilocks' porridge.

Gretel knew her brother too well. "We're going to be ok Hansel" she said reassuringly.

"But what if we die, what if we get captured again and there's no giant oven to save us? What if instead of going back to Dad and living happily ever after, this is it? This is where we die?" He threw his clip board angrily to the ground and ran off into the woods.

Gretel summoned the group and ran through the plan again. They couldn't fail. There was too much at stake. If Hansel didn't want to be part of the action, that was up to him.

Hansel slunk off into the woods, straying further and further away from the path. He stood on a large twig which cracked and echoed around the woods. The sun had disappeared, and the woods grew shadowy and dark. An owl hooted and Hansel started to run. He ran faster and faster, his heart pounding in his chest. He had to keep going. He had to find home – get help – before Gretel and the others became the next victims of the B.A.D. Network. He had to keep running. But he couldn't. He just couldn't. He fainted.

Meanwhile, the B.A.D network assembled – and what a sight they were to behold. A stinky old bridge troll, the big bad wolf with his gleaming white teeth, a man-eating giant, the cunning old fox, the evil stepmother and the wicked witch. They huddled together, swapping tales of lucky escapes and plotting the demise of Red, Hansel, Gretel and their friends.

Nearby, Gretel gave the signal. It was time for the brave group of friends to put their CRUSH THEM plan into action. For while these baddies might be the most evil, villainous members of the B.A.D. network, that didn't necessarily mean they were clever.

Lured in by the sweet smell of Goldilocks' porridge, the B.A.D. network didn't see the big sheet coming! Trapped underneath, the goats swung into action, tap dancing all over their B.A.D heads. Then Cinders fired up the catapult, pelting them with jellybeans until they

HURT. B.A.D members yelped and moaned underneath the sheet – dazed and confused by the cunning ambush.

Meanwhile, deep in the woods, Hansel woke up and SCREAMED. Right next to him sat a big, bad wolf, grinning up at him.

"My, what a loud scream you have! I was wondering when you would wake up,' said the wolf, rounding on Hansel.

Hansel was horrified at the sight of this beast and tried to scramble to his feet, but he slipped and fell back.

"Don't panic old bean. I just wondered if you'd like a snack. Your belly was rumbling in your sleep." Right on cue, Hansel's belly gave a loud rumble.

"Well, I am quite hungry actually, now you mention it," squeaked Hansel.

The wolf nudged him a plate of delicious berries and Hansel began eating them greedily, still eyeing the wolf with suspicion.

"Relax old fellow. I'm not one of those blood thirsty wolves that would eat you for lunch. I'm actually a vegetarian. I was deserted by my mother when I was only a pup, but Red took care of me, leaving a bowl of biscuits for me every day. She would also sing me to sleep – she has the sweetest voice. She was so kind to me that I decided never to eat humans again – I live on the berries and apples that grow near Red's house."

"So, you're really not going to eat me?" said Hansel, shovelling the berries into his mouth like they might be his last meal.

"Wouldn't dream of it," said the wolf. "But I am rather worried about Red. I haven't seen her for a few days – and I can smell swamp troll in the air, which always makes me nervous. Have you seen her?"

Hansel looked sheepish. He quickly told the wolf how the B.A.D network had chased them through forests, across fields, over rivers and down waterfalls – and that they'd been building an army of brave warriors to take down the network, once and for all.

"We must help them," said the wolf. "There's no time to lose. Hop on my back. Let's go!"

Hansel, filled with bravery (and berries) and inspired by the courage of his newfound vegetarian wolf friend, hopped onto his back and away they flew, back through the trees and into the clearing. And what a sight met their eyes!

Dangling from basketball hoops were the evil stepmother and the wicked witch. Dazed, confused and bruised, the giant and the troll huddled together crying and begging for mercy. The fox had eaten too much porridge and was being sick, while the big bad wolf was wrapped in a sheet and being pelted with jelly beans. 'Ow, ow, ow – please have mercy on us," he moaned. "We will turn over a new leaf – we promise. The B.A.D Network will be disbanded immediately."

Red, Gretel and the gang cheered, as they three little pigs put the finishing touches to the enormous brick tower. "You wouldn't know how to turn over a new leaf if you tried," said Red. "That's why we've built you a very special, custom-made tower – to keep you baddies together forever. We think you'll enjoy each other's company!"

Hansel and the wolf cheered. "You did it. The CRUSH THEM plan worked. Well done guys – I'm soooo proud of you!"

Gretel, shocked to see her brother with a huge wolf, turned the catapult towards them and took aim.

"NO!" said Red. "That's my wolf, Rodriguez. He's a harmless vegetarian."

Gretel looked at Hansel. He nodded. "It's true. Rodriguez found me in the woods and brought me back to you."

Gretel ran to Hansel and hugged him tight. "I'm glad you're ok brother. And I'm glad we did you proud. The plan definitely worked. The B.A.D Network are behind bars forever."

They whole gang had a big group hug – lots of high fives and chest bumps and woops and cheers. At last, the baddies were behind bars, where they belonged. And the friends were free to enjoy the forests, the fields, the rivers and the waterfalls again.

"It's time to head home," said Red. "Our work here is done."

"But we can't just leave the baddies out here all alone," said Hansel. "They'll starve."

"Good!" said Red. "It's what they deserve."

"It may be what they deserve" said Gretel, "...but we're better than that. Let's set up a rota. We can visit the Tower every week to give them fresh supplies."

The crew agreed that they'd each take it in turns to visit the Tower and ensure that the baddies had basic supplies.

They enjoyed one final group hug – proud of the role they'd each played in bringing down the B.A.D Network for good.

"I'll miss you guys," said Red as she hugged Hansel and Gretel.

"We'll be friends forever," said Gretel.

Hansel nodded his agreement - "But let's choose a safer adventure next time."

.

13

A twist in
the tale

Months went by, and the friends kept their word to visit the Tower every week with fresh supplies of food and other requests for the B.A.D Network.

One day, the wicked stepmother asked for ingredients to make gingerbread. It was the Giant's birthday and gingerbread was his favourite treat. Thinking nothing of it, Red brought all the ingredients – butter, sugar, flour, ginger, syrup, cinnamon and bicarbonate of soda.

"Enjoy your gingerbread!" she said, as she left to return home again.

Later that night, a loud BANG could be heard, sending tremors back over the waterfall, along the river, over the fields and through the forest.

When Gretel returned with fresh supplies, the Tower was no more. In its place – a pile of bricks and ash. As she looked closer, she saw footprints and pawprints in the ash, leading in all directions.

It could mean only one thing: The B.A.D. Network was on the loose once again!

About the Author

Berry Halpin is 10 years old and lives in North West London with her parents, her sister Cora and her bunnies, Marnie and Oreo. Berry started writing fiction in 2020 and is incredibly proud to launch her debut short story. Drawing on the themes and characters of well-known fairytales, Berry gives this story a unique 21st century twist, helping to reinvent the fairytale for the modern reader. When she's not writing, you can find her on the football pitch, climbing at Harrowall or camping in the great outdoors.

Acknowledgments

I'd like to thank my parents for introducing me to the stories and fairytales that fired my imagination for this book. I'd also like to thank my sister Cora – the ultimate companion in all my life's adventures.

-   *Berry Halpin, 2023*

.

Printed in Great Britain
by Amazon

37141655R00034